THE DADDY MOUNTAIN

JULES FEIFFER

MICHAEL DI CAPUA BOOKS • HYPERION BOOKS FOR CHILDREN

TO CHRIS

Watch me.

I'm getting ready to climb the Daddy Mountain.

It's very high.

But first I need something to drink.

**Fruit juice gives me energy to climb
the Daddy Mountain.**

**But first I have to put the empty glass in the sink
or my mother will get mad.**

I have to be brave.

I start by climbing the mountain's feet.

You have to be careful
or you could lose your balance.

I wrap my arms tight around a leg.

Then I stand on my tiptoes
and pull myself up.

Not too fast, though.

Because then
I might mess up.

And that could be
a catastrophe.

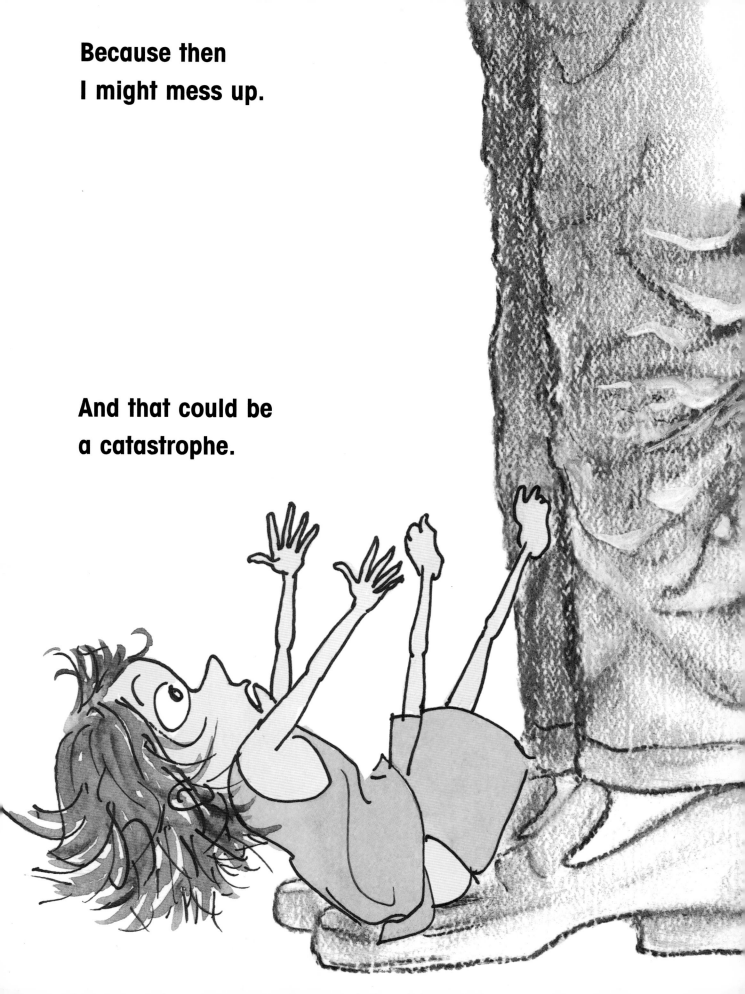

I have to be brave.

I crawl up a leg of
the Daddy Mountain.

I hold on tight
and go not too fast.

It's harder than you think.

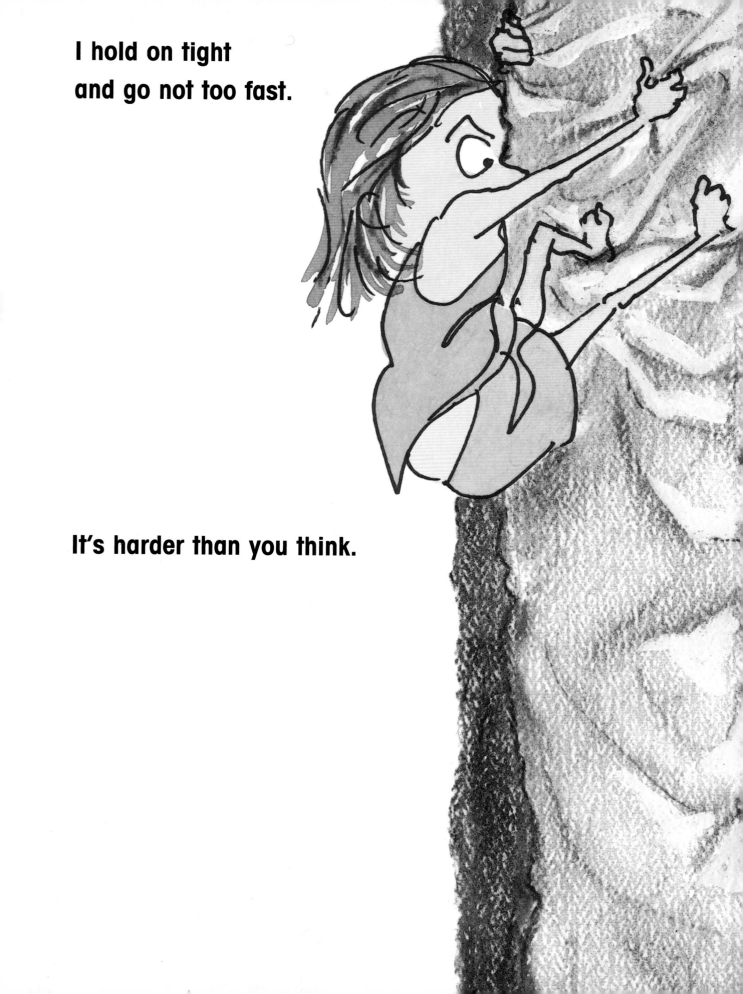

I reach the knees.
I need a rest.

The Daddy Mountain
has bony knees and
bends them for me
so I can sit and
catch my breath.

I don't want to dawdle.
I have to be brave.

I reach as high
as I can and
grab the belt of
the Daddy Mountain.

I pull myself up
with both hands.
I'm halfway!

Don't look down.

I have to be extra careful because of how high I am.

I could slip.

And that could be
a catastrophe.

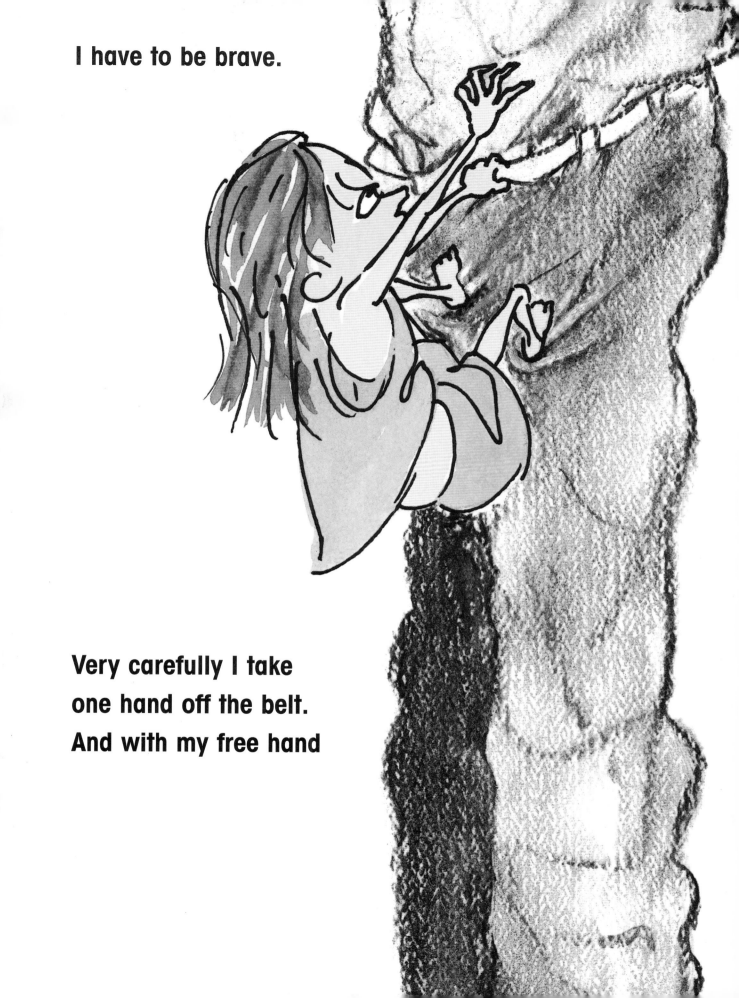

I have to be brave.

Very carefully I take
one hand off the belt.
And with my free hand

I grab a piece of shirt and pull myself up.
Remember, the Daddy Mountain must wear a shirt.

Because if you grab hold of his skin, he'll get mad.

Okay, two more grabs and I'm up to the collar.

Now this is
a tricky part,
also scary.

I swing one foot
wide as I can
onto a shoulder.

**Then the
other foot.**

So I'm kind of sitting on his shoulder
like it's a chair.

Very carefully, I start to stand up.
This is where I don't want to think too much.

I grab an ear.

This is no time to make a mistake.

Inches from the top! I can't believe I'm so brave.

I shout to my mother, "Come quick!"

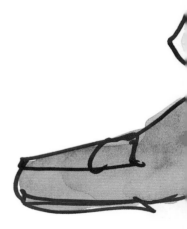

"I CLIMBED THE DADDY MOUNTAIN!"

I think she's going to faint.